Margaret Mahy

Tingleberries, Tuckertubs and Telephones

A Tale of Love and Ice-cream

Illustrated by Robert Staermose

SCHOLASTIC INC.

New York Toronto London Auckland Sydney
Mexico City New Delhi Hong Kong

ISBN 0-439-13755-1

Published by Scholastic Inc., 555 Broadway, New York, NY 10012, by arrangement with Puffin Books, a division of Penguin Putnam Inc. SCHOLASTIC and associated logos are trademarks and/or registered trademarks of Scholastic Inc.

12 11 10 9 8 7 6 5 4 3 2   9/9 0 1 2 3 4/0

Printed in the U.S.A.   40

First Scholastic printing, July 1999

Contents

Chapter 1

An Orphan on an Island

Saracen Hobday was a particularly shy orphan who lived on lonely Breakfast Island. He had lived on Breakfast Island for as long as he could remember, along with his dear old granny who loved him and gave him useful advice. 'Never waste good food, Saracen,' she would say over and over again, 'and never talk to strangers'. Saracen listened carefully, though it was particularly easy to take her advice because she was in charge of the cooking and no strangers ever came to Breakfast Island, anyway.

Saracen's granny had had a lot of practice telling other people what to do. Before becoming a dear old granny, she had been a detective inspector, famous throughout the great city of Hookywalker for catching villains. On her bedside table, between her bottle of Policeman's Foot Oil and her hairbrush, sat a blue velvet box holding a gold medal. This was the very medal she had received for capturing the pirate, Grudge-Gallows, along with his crew, his ship and all the treasure he had stolen.

When Saracen had been particularly good, he was allowed to polish this medal, and, as he did so, his granny would tell him, over and over again, stories of her great bravery.

'I'm modest to a fault, Saracen,' she would say, 'but one should always tell the truth, and I *was* the greatest detective inspector in Hookywalker. Some people praise Detective Inspector Cruddington, but, being utterly truthful, I have to admit I was much better and braver than he was.'

Apart from being a little on the bossy side, and telling the truth more than she absolutely had to, Saracen's granny was a good grandmother. She helped him dig in the sand when he was a baby and, as he grew older and wanted to dig in something more challenging than sand, she encouraged him to make his first garden. Actually, there wasn't much to do on Breakfast Island *except* gardening, but, in between gardening, Saracen and his grandmother ran up and down the long jetty that stuck out into Porridge Bay. Jetty-running doesn't sound all that exciting, but on Saracen's jetty it was quite thrilling because of the loose boards which flew up and hit anyone unlucky enough to step on them. Saracen, however, soon learned exactly which boards were loose, and leaped over them in perfect safety.

'I suppose I should nail those loose boards down,' said Saracen when his grandmother gave him a new hammer and a box of nails for his birthday. 'But, though I'm shy and can't bear to speak to strangers, I do like a little bit of danger in my life.'

'Quite right!' said his grandmother. 'A bit of danger gingers up everyday life, and I like life with plenty of ginger in it.'

Chapter 2

A Limp Lettuce Leaf in the Great Salad of Life

As well as all the ginger of the jetty, Saracen and his dear old granny had a lovely garden, two huge glass-houses, and a herd of black-and-white cows which gave plenty of milk for home-made ice-cream. Yet, in spite of making ice-cream, leaping up and down the jetty, digging in the garden, and keeping an eye on her grandson, Saracen's granny couldn't help longing for new adventures. Deep down, she missed being a detective inspector and chasing after Grudge-Gallows. The only problem with having a gold medal is that once you have one, you feel it would be nice to have two or three more. And she hated the thought that her old rival, Detective Inspector Cruddington, might be having a dangerous and exciting time catching villains, while she had to leap up and down the jetty in order to have any sort of adventure at all. These days, alas, all glory seemed to lie in the distant past. The only contact Granny had with Hookywalker was through the old black telephone in the hall, or the Baconville Launch Service, an ancient boat which called in once a day. It puttered up to the end of the jetty, tossed off a newspaper (along with anything else ordered from Hookywalker), and puttered straight off again.

The arrival of the Baconville launch was the great event of the day. Of course, it was Granny who had to leap down the jetty to catch the newspaper or collect anything the captain of the launch happened to bring them, for Saracen was so terribly shy. As soon as the launch came putt-puttering through the Marmalade Heads, Saracen shinned up a pohutukawa tree and wouldn't come down until the launch had putt-puttered off again. All he ever saw of the captain was the top of a gold-braided hat, glimpsed through lots of twigs and leaves.

'What does the captain look like, Granny?' he sometimes asked when the launch was well out of sight.

'Oh, Saracen,' his grandmother would reply impatiently. 'Find out for yourself. I know I've taught you not to speak to strangers, but I never dreamed you would take me quite so literally. How will you ever make a fortune, or fall in love, if you climb a tree every time a boat comes through the Marmalade Heads?'

'Fall in love!' cried Saracen indignantly. 'I'm not the sort of fellow who ever falls in love!'

But his grandmother went on nagging him.

'Do you think I would have won a medal with my name on it if I had climbed a tree every time I saw a villain like Grudge-Gallows?' she demanded.

'I just can't help it, Granny,' sighed Saracen. 'The thought of talking to a stranger, even over the telephone, makes me feel like a mere limp lettuce leaf in the great salad of life.'

You can tell from these words that, though Saracen wasn't likely to become a great detective inspector, he was a bit of a poet as well as being a keen gardener.

Chapter 3

Ha! Ha! Ha!

One day, Saracen watched his granny bounding lightly down the jetty (just as usual), reading the newspaper (which the captain of the launch had thrown into her outstretched hands), and jumping over the loose boards (which she could do without looking up from her reading, because she knew exactly where they all were). Suddenly, she came to a dead standstill, which is the stillest kind of standstill known to science. A hoarse cry of horror rose from behind the newspaper.

'Grudge-Gallows has escaped,' Granny yelled. 'This is terrible! Oh! It says here that he secretly knitted himself a ladder. It says here that he sewed himself a pirate flag during the prison sewing classes. Last night a thunderstorm struck Hookywalker and put out all the street lights. Grudge-Gallows flung his knitted ladder across the prison wall. Up and over and off he ran, straight to the Hookywalker wharf. Oh, Saracen! It says here that he has stolen his old ship, *Pirate Promise*, from the

Hookywalker Wharf Museum. What wickedness! And that's not all. He has also stolen a cell phone from the Wharf Museum Office and left a mocking note saying, *"I am off to the Antarctic. Catch me if you can, Detective Inspector! Ha! Ha! Ha!"'*

At that exact moment, they both heard the old black phone ringing in the hall. The cows in the paddock beside the glass-house looked up, full of lazy curiosity, but Saracen's grandmother was off the jetty, across the beach, and in through the door in three leaps, acting more like a kangaroo than a woman of the world. Saracen followed rather more slowly.

'Just as I thought,' cried Granny to Saracen, waving the receiver at him as he reached the veranda. 'That was the Government on the phone! Detective Inspector Cruddington is chasing bandits in the Jackrabbit Desert. It's me they want. *Me!* I am to set off after Grudge-Gallows immediately. Oh, Saracen, I'm off to the Antarctic, so listen carefully. The deep-freeze is jam-packed full

of ice-cream and sausages, but if you need anything from the mainland you'll have to ring for it.
You know how to do that, don't you?'

'What? Talk to a stranger?' Saracen cried.
'Granny, I'm much too shy.'

'Now, pull yourself together, Saracen,' his
grandmother exclaimed, searching in the side-
board drawer for her detective inspector's badge.
'I'm sorry, Saracen, but you can see it is most
important that I catch that villain Grudge-Gallows
as quickly as possible, or they might give
Cruddington the job. Luckily, I have many
albatross friends, so we'll be able to stay in touch
even though there are no telephone boxes or post
offices in the Antarctic. Now, I must take my bottle
of Policeman's Foot Oil. And I'll wear my gold
medal, too.'

Chapter 4

Goodbye, Granny!

After the first shock Saracen found, to his secret surprise, that he was rather looking forward to living on Breakfast Island with no dear old granny to boss him about.

'I'll be able to garden the way *I* want to,' he thought. 'I'll plant the lettuces in a different place, for one thing.'

And this daring decision made him feel that he might even overcome his fear of using the old black phone. Why, if he had to, he might just bring himself to leap down the jetty as the launch came putt-puttering in past the Burnt Toast Rocks, and catch the newspaper for himself (though the captain of the launch had a particularly good aim, and almost never threw the newspaper into the sea).

However, in spite of these dreams, Saracen was still far too shy to meet the launch when it made a special trip that very afternoon to collect his grandmother. She was waiting impatiently on the end of the jetty, with her Policeman's Foot Oil, her snow shoes, and other vital detective-inspector equipment neatly packed in a basket beside her.

'Goodbye, Saracen!' she shouted, waving cheerfully at the pohutukawa tree.

'Goodbye, Granny,' Saracen yelled, waving back.

All his granny could see of her dear grandson, as she slid a goodbye glance down Porridge Bay, was a flapping hand sticking out from among the leaves of the pohutukawa tree.

Chapter 5

A Peculiar Plant in a Plastic Bag

Saracen missed his granny almost at once, but he found he enjoyed missing her. He was able to do all sorts of things without her looking over his shoulder and telling him how to do them better. He fished in his own way from the end of the jetty, gathered fruit and vegetables in his own way from the garden, and helped himself in his own way to ice-cream from the deep-freeze. There was nobody to tell him that too much ice-cream would chill his stomach and that he must put half of it back. Life was wonderful.

Of course, Saracen *did* miss having someone to talk to. He was still far too shy to use the phone. And he watched a little wistfully from the pohutukawa tree whenever the captain tossed a rolled-up newspaper on to the end of the jetty, and putt-puttered off again.

Days turned into weeks. Then, one after another, giant albatrosses began bringing letters from Granny, all of which they dropped neatly on the front-door mat. Saracen was able to mark her progress with coloured pins on the map of the Antarctic he had tacked up on the kitchen wall. She had reached King Edward VII Land, and conducted a full investigation. She had put to sea again and gone on to Wrigley Gulf. So far, there was nothing to report. She hoped Saracen was looking after himself and the cows and the garden, and warned him about the dangers of eating too much

ice-cream. 'Always leave the table feeling you could eat a little more,' was her good advice. 'But, Saracen, never waste food!'

One lovely sunny day an albatross turned up, carrying not only a letter but a small bundle wrapped in plastic. The sagacious bird carefully dropped both the bundle and the letter on the door mat before taking off once more in a southerly direction.

'Another letter from Granny! Perhaps she's caught Grudge-Gallows. Perhaps she's on her way home,' Saracen cried, snatching up the bundle and tearing it open.

Inside the plastic bag he found a lot of half-melted snow, and cuttings of a strange plant doing its best to blossom among ice crystals. Drops of water dripped like chilly tears from the ends of its petals.

'What does this mean?' Saracen muttered, tearing open the letter. 'Is it a clue of some kind? And what kind of plant is it? I've never seen anything like it before.'

Chapter 6

News from the Middle of a Snowstorm

Dear Saracen (the letter began),

Go to the map of the Antarctic on the kitchen wall and put a small flag in the middle of the Hollick Kenyon plateau. Now, imagine a snowstorm raging all around that flag! And imagine me in the middle of the middle of that snowstorm, for that is where I am. I haven't caught up with Grudge-Gallows yet, but I think he might be making for the Filchner Ice Shelf, so I am taking a dangerous short cut overland (something Cruddington would never dare to do. He is a mere desert detective and totally useless when it comes to ice). Thank all the stars for Policeman's Foot Oil! Anyhow, going for a short, refreshing stroll through the snow last night, I came upon this hitherto unknown Antarctic plant, and I am sending you some cuttings by the albatross network. Importing unknown plants can sometimes be dangerous, but, living on an island, you will be able to keep

it in quarantine. It loves snowstorms, so pop it straight into our deep-freeze. If it survives the shock of being transplanted, you will be the only gardener in the world to own this gallant plant. I call it the tingleberry.

Your affectionate grandmother

PS: I notice it grows rather a lot of berries. They are not poisonous. Eat them all so as not to waste food or hurt the plant's feelings.

Chapter 7

Tingleberries

Saracen glanced anxiously at the tingleberry cuttings. They were weeping sadly in the warm breezes of Breakfast Island, so he pushed them into his breakfast bowl of ice-cream. Instantly the plant revived. Its melting petals grew crisp and icy. It even put out four new leaves. Saracen decided to shut it safely in the freezer.

'What will I do with it next?' he wondered. 'The freezer is going to be much too small for a plant used to the vast, icy wastes of the Antarctic. I know! I shall turn one of the glass-houses into a frost-house.' Saracen did a little dance, delighted by his own good idea. Then he stopped and frowned. 'But that will mean getting a new refrigerator . . . an enormous one. And *that* will mean ringing Hookywalker and talking to a – urrgh! – to a *stranger*.' For a moment his knees went all weak and wavery, and his voice faded to a mere whimpering whisper. But then he thought of the gallant tingleberry and the way it had put out a few hopeful leaves. It was relying on him to do his best.

Saracen was a dedicated gardener. He cleared the whimper out of his throat and forced his knees to stiffen themselves. 'That tingleberry needs friendship and loving care,' he said in a voice that now echoed boldly from the refrigerator door. 'This is a moment of truth. I can . . . I must . . . I *will* be brave.'

Chapter 8

Saracen is Struck by Love

Searching in the pages of the telephone book, Saracen soon found a likely business called *Jack's Frigid-Air Service*. Then he dialled the number very, very carefully. His heart thumped like a bongo drum as he waited. Breakfast Island didn't have access to direct dialling, and he knew his call would have to go through an operator in Baconville. The thought of actually having to listen to a stranger's voice made him want to hide under the table. But Saracen was determined to make life as happy as possible for the tingleberry.

'Name and number, please,' the operator sang down the line. Saracen was electrified.

The operator had the most beautiful voice in the world. Saracen was utterly overwhelmed by the sheer music of it. He couldn't say a word.

'Name and number, please,' she repeated, her voice sounding even more beautiful the second time than it had the first. But something extraordinary had happened to Saracen . . . something he

had always sworn would never, ever happen to *him*.

'I've been struck down by love,' he thought in horror. 'I knew it was risky to use the telephone, but I didn't realize just how dangerous it was.' He whispered his number and listened eagerly.

'Through now!' sang the operator. The line buzzed and clicked and Saracen's call was put through to Hookywalker.

'Jack here! What can I do you for?' said a voice at the other end of the line. Saracen had to pull himself together. Whispering shyly, he ordered an enormous refrigerator, and asked Jack to send it over to him that very afternoon on the Baconville launch.

Then he went out to his garden. He hoped that digging over last year's potato patch would calm his nerves, but during the entire morning, whether Saracen was turning the potato patch or laying weeds neatly on the compost heap, the words, 'Name and number please!' rang in his head like golden bells.

Chapter 9

The Tingleberries Take Off

Putt-putt-putt-putt went the Baconville launch as it headed into Porridge Bay. Saracen watched from behind the pohutukawa tree as the captain operated the little crane on the back of the launch, skilfully swinging the huge fridge on to the end of the jetty. As the launch putt-puttered back around the Burnt Toast Rocks, Saracen was already picking up that fridge with his front-end loader and sweeping it towards his glass-houses, weaving skilfully in and out among the grazing cows. It was the work of a moment for a handyman like Saracen to connect the fridge to the nearest glass-house. Frost immediately formed inside the glass, and Saracen ran to his kitchen fridge to collect the tingleberry cuttings. To his amazement, the freezer door had been pushed open by tingleberry shoots which were twisting out of it in all directions. Some were even flowering. Those tingleberries had taken off like ice-rockets.

Saracen quickly transplanted them to the new frost-house, carefully digging in lots of ice-cream around their roots. By the time he left the frost-house the tingleberries were putting out shy tendrils and beginning to climb the walls.

Over the next two days, though Saracen worked late and long ice-creaming the tingleberries, the magical words, 'Name and number, please!' and, 'Through now!' sang in his head. Petals of ice fell from the tingleberry flowers with a musical tinkle, and little tingleberries immediately began to form. They looked exactly like ice-creams in pointed pink cones. Saracen's granny had told him that it was

quite safe to eat them, so he carefully tried his first tingleberry. What joy! It tasted like rich ice-cream with sweet berries beaten into it . . . the best ice-cream you could possibly imagine. Saracen stepped back with a sigh of pleasure. Then he looked at his vines and frowned. There were already so many tingleberries – hundreds of them. A mere man on his own, no matter how passionately he loved ice-cream, could not possibly eat all of them, yet good food, he knew, must not go to waste.

'Name and number, please?' sang the sweet voice in his memory. 'Through now!'

Suddenly, Saracen had an idea. He would phone the Baconville operator and ask for advice. He would not only hear her wonderful voice once more, but he might get some good quality assistance, too.

Chapter 10

Struck Down by Love Again

Saracen made up a phone number, ran to the phone, and dialled it.

'I am sorry, but that number doesn't exist,' sang the operator's voice, sounding even more beautiful than he had remembered it. Saracen blushed so furiously that his ears lit up like Christmas lights.

'It was you I wanted to talk to. I need some advice,' he whispered. 'And, since my granny is still chasing Grudge-Gallows all over the Antarctic, you are the only person I can turn to.'

'Telephone operators love being helpful,' said the beautiful voice. 'Ask away!'

'My tingleberry vines are producing far too many tingleberries,' said Saracen. 'I don't want to waste them, but I can't eat them all. What should I do?'

'That's easy! Harvest the tingleberries and send them to the fruit and flower market in Hookywalker,' suggested the lovely voice on the Baconville end of the line.

'Thank you! Thank you!' Saracen said sincerely. 'I shall always treasure your wonderful advice.

Please put me through to the fruit and flower market at once.'

'Through now!' sang the Baconville operator.

That very afternoon, watching from high in his usual tree as the Baconville launch putt-puttered past the Marmalade Heads, Saracen had a sudden, disturbing thought.

'What will the captain do when he finds an unexpected consignment of tingleberries, packed in ice and addressed to the Hookywalker fruit and flower market, waiting on the end of the jetty?' he wondered. 'I'd better tell him to keep them out of direct sunlight.'

Filled with a new courage born of love and the natural excitement of a man starting a business, Saracen leaped bravely down the jetty, missing every loose plank with remarkable skill, and blushing deeply so that, from a distance, he looked a little like a bounding traffic light.

Then a terrifying thing happened. A fresh sea breeze blew the captain's hat into the water. Brown curls tumbled out from under it. The captain of the launch was a girl! There was no doubt about it. Saracen had seen pictures of girls in the newspaper, and he recognized one immediately. This

girl's curls were a dark muffin-brown, and her skin was a light muffin-brown and her eyes were almost certainly brown as well. She was too busy trying to fish her gold-braided captain's hat out of the sea to notice Saracen, but Saracen saw her quite plainly.

At once, he doubled up with an attack of shyness. Pretending to hear the phone ringing in his house, he spun round, bolted down the jetty, burst in at his back door, and bundled himself under the table. Here he stayed, with his eyes shut, until he heard the sound of the launch putt-puttering out past the Burnt Toast Rocks, taking his tingleberries to Baconville where they would connect with the Hookywalker Refrigerated Transport Service.

As he came out from under the table, Saracen realized that for a second time that day, he had been struck by the full force of love.

Chapter 11

In Touch with the World

'How can it be? I am already in love with the Baconville phone operator,' he thought. 'I'd better remind myself just how beautiful her voice is. I know! I'll ring her and ask for some more advice about something.'

Hastily, he ran to the phone.

But the voice that answered him this time was not the one he was longing to hear. It was the voice of an answering service, flat and disappointing.

'All lines out of Baconville are busy at the moment. Please wait patiently. You are in the priority queue. We will connect you as soon as possible.' Music started. Saracen did as he was told and waited patiently.

He waited for half an hour. Then the music stopped abruptly and he heard the operator's sweet tones saying, 'Name and number, please!'

'Thank goodness! You *are* there,' cried Saracen. 'I need advice urgently.'

'What can I do to help you?' asked the voice. Saracen found he was much too shy to explain that he had fallen in love not only with her, but with the captain of the Baconville launch, as well.

'I . . . I still have far too many tingleberries on my tingleberry vines,' he stammered, which was perfectly true. 'What can I possibly do with them?'

'I shall connect you with fruit and flower markets overseas,' said the voice. 'You never know. Tingleberries might become wildly popular in foreign parts. You might be able to set up a flourishing export business. Through now!'

Saracen was so enchanted by the words, 'Through now!' that he barely heard the ring-ring of the phone connecting him across thousands of miles of ocean to the fruit and flower market in a distant city in a faraway country. 'I really do love that beautiful voice,' he thought to himself. But then he remembered the captain's wild and wind-tossed curls. Horrakapotchkin! Saracen Hobday, the shyest boy in the world (someone who had promised himself and his dear old granny that he would never fall in love under any circumstances), was in love with two women at one and the same time, and on the same day, too. One of them he had heard but never seen, and the other he had seen but never heard. Horrakapotchkin twice over!

'This is the Fruit and Vegetable Market in Sydney,' said an Australian voice at the other end of the phone.

'Concentrate on gardening,' Saracen muttered to himself, and he talked eloquently about tingleberries for ten minutes. Then he scribbled down an order from Sydney for a couple of boxes of tingleberries (to be sent by launch and truck to the nearest airport). And after that he went out into his frost-house to dig more ice-cream in around the roots of his plants. This hard work cooled him down and warmed him up at one and the same time, and the tingleberries enjoyed it, too.

Chapter 12

A Succulent Tomato in the Great
Salad of Life

Over the next few days tingleberries suddenly became the most popular fruit in Hooky-walker, and within a fortnight they were the most

popular fruit in the world. They had a cold, creamy taste that everyone simply adored. Saracen's old black phone was never silent. Market Managers rang from distant countries demanding that he put cartons of tingleberries on the Baconville launch. Huge trucks began clustering at the Baconville wharf so that they could rush tingleberries to the Hookywalker airport.

By the following Thursday, when Saracen counted his money, he was amazed at just how rich he had suddenly become. Not only that, his frosthouse was overflowing with a new crop of tingleberries, while the phone kept ringing from fruit and flower markets all over the world. Every caller said the same thing. *Please rush us a hundred cartons of tingleberries as soon as possible.*

Saracen began to feel he was a succulent tomato in the great salad of life. However, it was all too much for his old black telephone. Late on Friday morning, it suddenly fell to pieces.

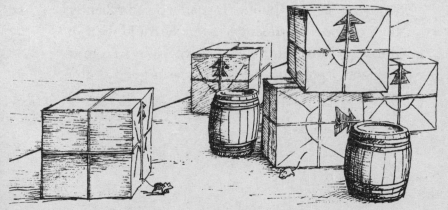

Chapter 13

A Gold Telephone Studded with Diamonds

The Baconville operator immediately contacted the phone company, and Saracen was sent a new phone on the Baconville launch, along with a pretty card congratulating him on being such an outstanding customer. 'We are sending you our executive phone,' the card said. 'It is solid gold and studded with diamonds. It should suit a man of your standing.'

'Standing?' thought Saracen. 'I don't just stand. I dig and leap as well. And I'm always running backwards and forwards.' He was too shy, though, to ring the telephone company and put them right on these points. Deep down, he couldn't help enjoying his new phone. It sparkled so brilliantly that, provided the door was open, he could see it all the way from the far end of the jetty. From a gardener's point of view it was just as good as any gold medal.

Chapter 14

Popular but Puzzled

Bᵘᵗ Saracen, though suddenly rich and popular, was also deeply puzzled.

'Am I having a good time or a bad time?' Saracen asked himself. 'I have suddenly grown rich and that's a good thing. But then I have also fallen in love with two beautiful women at the same time, and that is a bad thing. Of course, I am now the owner of a solid gold telephone studded with diamonds. That's a good thing. But what use is a golden telephone when you have no friends to talk to? No friends is a bad thing. I *do* have a dear old granny, and that's a good thing, but she is a detective inspector and has had to go off to the Antarctic to hunt for the terrible pirate, Grudge-Gallows, and that is a bad thing. If she knew I had this solid gold telephone she would ring me – and that's a good thing. But then, even if she did know, there are no telephone boxes in the Antarctic. Now, that's a bad thing. Oh dear, life has become so complicated over the last two weeks.'

Trying to work out whether things were good or

bad, Saracen picked up the telephone directory,
and idly leafed through its pages.

An unexpected poem in elegant, curly print caught his eye.

'Pizza fit for any King.
Ring our number! Ring! Ring! Ring!
In a tree? Or underground?
We will rush a pizza round
At any time of night or day.
All you have to do is pay!

Hungry Harry's is the place
For pizza that will fill your face.
Pizza to your very door.
Hookywalker 554.'

'I've never dialled for pizza before,' Saracen murmured, 'and now that I have a new, solid gold telephone, this is the time to begin. Of course, I do live on Breakfast Island, and *Hungry Harry*'s *is* in Hookywalker. But now I am so rich I can afford to have a pizza delivered, even if it does have to come out to the island on a launch.'

Chapter 15

Saracen Dials the Wrong Number

Saracen muttered *Hungry Harry*'s number, blushing at the thought of speaking to the operator he loved. But love often makes people careless. Saracen muttered the wrong number. And then he actually *dialled* it.

'Thank you, Saracen! Through now!' trilled the beautiful voice. Saracen wondered if she could hear the beating of his heart, reverberating like bongo drums, over the line.

'I've been in love for more than a fortnight now,' he muttered impatiently. 'When does it begin to wear off?' *Boom biddy boom biddy, bing bang bong,* went his heart. Then, many, many miles away he heard someone's voice answering the telephone.

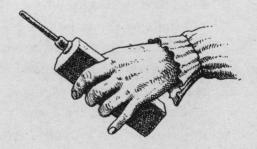

47

Chapter 16

A Gritty, Gravelly, Gravy Voice

A rich, rough voice answered him. It sounded like the voice of someone who had been eating gritty gravel mixed with gravy.

'Who do you think you're a-dialling of?' this gravelly, gravy voice groaned gruffly. 'It's midnight, and we sea-dogs need our beauty sleep.'

'Is that *Hungry Harry's Pizza Delivery Service*?' asked Saracen.

'No, it isn't! Never!' yelled the voice. 'Don't insult us or you'll be sorry! Our vengeance will be terrible.'

'I'm sorry already,' Saracen said hastily. 'I'm not quite used to this new solid gold phone of mine. I must have dialled the wrong number.' Saracen was not quite as shy as he had been the week before, and he couldn't resist boasting about his new phone. 'You see, it is studded with diamonds and it *is* rather dazzling.'

'Gold phone?' cried the rough voice. 'Did I understand you properly? Are you really talking into a new, solid gold phone set with *diamonds*?'

'It was a present from the phone company,' explained Saracen. 'Just recently, I have been phoning so many fruit and flower markets all over the world that my old black phone fell to pieces.'

'A solid gold telephone, eh?' said the gritty, gravelly, gravy voice greedily. 'Studded with diamonds, eh? Well, we sea-dogs might just drop in on you!'

Saracen was filled with alarm and excitement at

the thought of unexpected visitors. This time last week he would have dropped the phone and hidden under the table, but now, what with all the practice he had had telephoning, he thought he just might manage to put up with a few visitors.

'Please call in,' he said politely. 'I have to work long hours in my frost-house, digging ice-cream in around the roots of the tingleberries, but I'll take time off to make you a cup of tea. I live in Porridge Bay on Breakfast Island. You come through the Marmalade Heads, past the Burnt Toast Rocks. Don't be offended if I climb a pohutukawa tree when I see you coming up the long jetty. Just stand around talking about the weather until I get used to the idea of visitors, and climb down again. I think it might take about half an hour.'

But whoever it was whose number Saracen had dialled by mistake gave a sinister laugh.

'You would be right to hide from us, shipmate,' the gravelly voice cried, 'for we're not mere visitors. At this exact moment you are a-talking to the famous pirate captain, Grudge-Gallows, and after I have put this phone down I'm going to point our ship towards Breakfast Island, and close in on that golden telephone of yours. Ha! Ha! A golden telephone! We had our last treasure chest taken by a detective inspector, and it's time we built up a new hoard.'

WANTED

GABRIEL GRUDGE-GALLOWS
~: *THE FIERCEST PIRATE IN THE WORLD* :~

FOR
PILLAGING, PLUNDERING & PIRACY

* <u>REWARD</u> *

Grudge-Gallows! The fiercest pirate in the world! And where was Detective Inspector Granny? Somewhere out in the Antarctic rubbing Policeman's Foot Oil between her toes? Horrakapotchkin!

'I didn't know pirates had telephones,' stammered Saracen.

'We're modern *executive* pirates. We have cell phones,' growled Grudge-Gallows.

There was a click. Grudge-Gallows had hung-up.

'Who would have thought that owning a telephone could be so adventurous,' cried Saracen, staring into the receiver. 'I have become suddenly rich. I've fallen in love two times over, and now pirates are pointing their ship at me!'

Chapter 17

Hanging-up on Granny

The golden telephone rang.

'Hello,' cried Saracen. 'Look, I can't talk now! I have to go out and prepare for a pirate attack.'

'Saracen,' cried the voice at the other end of the line. 'It's Granny here. I was caught on an iceberg and accidentally drifted north. A fishing boat with a radio telephone has just rescued me, so I am able to speak to you at last. How are you managing?'

'Oh, Granny, I have fallen in love twice over, *and* made a fortune, and now I'm about to be attacked by Grudge-Gallows. Life is almost too exciting.'

'Grudge-Gallows!' exclaimed Granny. 'Do you mean that while I've been trekking across the Antarctic through storms and blizzards, Grudge-Gallows has been skulking around Breakfast Island? All that trekking for nothing but tricking? Never mind! I'll call on a few albatross friends and be at your side as soon as possible. In the meantime, hide under the bed.'

'No, Granny,' said Saracen, amazed to find he

wanted to outwit Grudge-gallows all by himself. 'It is my job to protect the cows and the tingleberries, as well as my solid gold telephone.'

'Saracen, this is not just your grandmother speaking, this is an experienced detective inspector. Don't make things complicated for the police. Go to your room and get under the bed at once,' shouted Granny.

But Saracen had already hung up.

Almost at once, he was shocked at what he had done.

He had not only hung up on his grandmother, he had hung up on a detective inspector as well. Yet, as he thought about it, he began to feel rather proud of himself. 'If I can hang up on a grandmother, it shows I am brave enough to take on Grudge-Gallows,' he thought. 'Now, let me think for a moment! What am I good at? Digging and leaping and using the phone. Right! I'll do all three, one after the other, and maybe all at the same time.'

Chapter 18

Pirate Attack

For the rest of the morning Saracen was extremely busy with the digging part of his plan. Suddenly, he straightened up sharply. The sound of rough singing came wafting faintly across the water. *Pirate Promise*, a fine vessel with sails as well as a huge outboard motor, came chugging gracefully through the Marmalade Heads, just grazing the Burnt Toast Rocks. From its mast waved the pirate flag, a beautiful example of prison school embroidery. The breeze brought the words of a defiant pirate song clearly to his ears.

'Fifteen men on a red cell phone!
Yo! Ho! Ho! We've escaped from jail.
Fifteen hearts as hard as stone!
Ring! Ring! Ring! And we're on your trail.
Flags are tattooed on our backs.
(Smiling skulls and criss-crossed bones!)
Do not ring or send a fax!
Just surrender all gold phones.
Do not howl or shout for help!
There's nothing anyone can do.

Give in with a despairing yelp,
And don't call us. We're calling you.'

Quickly, Saracen ran inside to his golden phone.
The beautiful voice of the Baconville operator
answered his urgent ring.
    'Name and number, please!'
    'This is 10! You know! Breakfast Island. Saracen
Hobday.'

'Oh, Saracen, you sound so brave this morning. I was about to go for lunch, but now you've rung me, may I help you?'

'Yes, you certainly can! I am about to fight Grudge-Gallows and his entire pirate crew. Could you please tell the captain of the launch that my prisoners will all be tied up on the end of the jetty? She will need a big net to hold them all, when she's lifting them into the back of the launch with her crane.'

'But Saracen . . . who's going to help you capture all those pirates?' cried the lovely voice, sounding most concerned.

'I'm going to do it all myself!' boasted Saracen. 'Though I am shy, I am particularly strong, what with gardening and swinging up into the tree for hiding purposes. Besides, though shy, I am particularly brave. Did you know you can be shy and brave at the same time? I am, though I didn't know it was possible until early this morning.'

'You certainly sound a lot braver than most people,' said the beautiful voice. 'But you will need help with a monster like Grudge-Gallows, and I shall help you. I shall go to lunch now.'

The line went dead.

'Odd!' thought Saracen, staring at the silent receiver. 'How will it help me if she goes to lunch?' However, he didn't have time to worry about that.

For *Pirate Promise* was almost at the jetty, with pirates leaning over the side and clinging to the rigging, yelling blood-curdling threats.

Saracen put down the receiver. Then he unplugged the golden phone and ran down to the beach, under the pohutukawa tree, and almost to the end of the jetty.

'Here it is!' he shouted, waving the phone so that it glittered richly in the sunlight. 'Come and get it – if you dare!'

A howl went up from the pirates at the sight of the golden phone. They couldn't even be bothered to drop anchor. Led by Grudge-Gallows himself, they all leaped over the side of *Pirate Promise* and raced down the jetty after Saracen.

Chapter 19

Hot Peppers in the
Great Salad of Life

Off went Saracen, only just ahead of the pirates, holding the golden phone above his head which he wiggled in a teasing fashion, and leaping over all the loose boards as he came to them.

'Catch him! Catch him!' howled Grudge-Gallows. But as he spoke – swish-bang! swish-bang! – loose boards punched upwards in every-whichever-way. Left! Right! Some pirates were struck far out to sea like well-hit cricket balls. Others dropped to the jetty, utterly stunned. Grudge-Gallows himself had his nose flattened, but he was so tough, he barely hesitated. Such a bang merely whipped him into a state of fury.

'After him!' he shouted to his remaining buccaneers. 'We are hot peppers in the great salad of life. Revenge! Revenge!'

Saracen reached the end of the jetty. At the sound of the sand gritting under his gardening boots, he gathered himself like a coiled steel spring, then . . . wheeeee . . . he gave a leap that would have won him a gold medal at any kangaroo Olympics. Not one of the pirates could jump like

that. They all crashed off the jetty – landing on the sand at the exact spot Saracen had planned – the very place where he had spent most of the morning digging a deep pirate pit. He had covered the whole with dried fronds from the tingleberries, before covering them with sand and shells. The pit came as a complete surprise to the pirates, who crashed into it, yelling with terror.

'Ha ha! Got you!' shouted Saracen. But this mocking cry was a bad mistake. It spurred the pirates to action, even though they were all severely bruised and had sand in their eyes. 'Fling the king! Fling the king! One, two, three!' they began chanting, hoisting the biggest, angriest pirate of them all up out of the pit, and on to the sand.

And guess which pirate it was . . . Yes! That particularly hot pepper, Grudge-Gallows himself!

Chapter 20

A Poisonous Promise by a
Pernicious Pirate

'You will suffer for this,' bellowed Grudge-Gallows. 'I'm going to disconnect you! I'm going to chop down your telegraph pole, hack up your jetty, and carry off your golden telephone.'

Saracen was already skimming across the field next to the paddock that held the frost-house. To tell you the truth, he *was* a little worried. He had somehow thought that his deep sandpit would catch every single pirate. Yet Grudge-Gallows had not only escaped from the sandpit, he was now in peppery pursuit and about to grab him. Saracen vaulted over the fence, glancing around anxiously as he did so. From the corner of his eye he caught a glimpse of a small dark cloud travelling rapidly over the sea towards him. A flash of lightning played over its surface.

'It's going to rain!' Saracen thought despairingly. 'Everything happens all at once.'

Grudge-Gallows, now right behind him, put out a huge, hairy hand. Saracen could feel fingers as

big as sausages brushing his shirt collar.

At this moment the cows, who were all on Saracen's side, joined in the chase. One of them prodded Grudge-Gallows' bottom with her horns. It is well known that all pirates, even the fiercest ones, are alarmed by cows with horns. In fact, one of the reasons they go to sea in the first place is to get away from cows with horns. Grudge-Gallows certainly hadn't bargained with having his bottom prodded. He was distracted.

Saracen leaped another fence, gaining a yard or two. Somewhere behind him the cow gave a disappointed 'Mooo!'. Grudge-Gallows had bounced right over the fence, even though it was made of barbed wire. The sound of pounding pirate feet closed in on Saracen all over again.

As they ran past the frost-house, something terrible happened. Grudge-Gallows let out a triumphant cry.

'Stop! Stop!' he shouted. 'Stop, or I'll open the door of the frost-house. Stop, or I'll let the cold air out and the sunshine in.'

At the thought of the sunshine falling on his precious tingleberries, Saracen skidded to a stand-still.

Grudge-Gallows had one hand on the handle of the frost-house door. In the other he held vital cables that connected the frost-house to the big fridge – the very fridge which had caused Saracen to use the phone for the first time.

'Ha! Ha! Ha!' Grudge Gallows cried. 'Surrender that phone or all your tingleberries will die!'

'Don't unplug my tingleberries,' begged Saracen. 'They were a present from my old granny! Are you the sort of man who would disconnect a grandmother's humble gift to her only grandson?'

'Throw that golden phone to me,' said Grudge-Gallows, 'and I promise your tingleberries will survive.' He was completely merciless.

Saracen sighed. But he knew that he was beaten, and he flung the telephone over to the wicked pirate. How beautifully it glittered as it flew through the air!

The telephone company will never trust me with another golden phone, he thought sadly. But, after all, the phone is mere gold, whereas the tingleberries are part of the rich salad of life.

'Aha!' shouted Grudge-Gallows, catching the golden phone with one hand, even though it was extremely heavy. 'You silly gardener. Never rely on promises from a peppery pirate! I am going to disconnect your fridge *and* open the frost-house door, anyway. Ha! Ha! Ha! Ha!'

'Don't you dare!' shouted a voice. A shadow slid over the late-afternoon sun. The cloud Saracen had glimpsed earlier was now hovering overhead. But it wasn't a cloud. It was his grandmother being carried through the air by seven great albatrosses. The medal on her chest flashed like lightning. She was suspended by bird power, just above Grudge-Gallows.

'You fiend! You fraud! You riddle-diddle-dumpling!' she cried. 'At last I've found you. I charge you with telephone theft, cruelty to plants, and uttering hollow threats.'

Chapter 21

Just in Time

G rudge-Gallows glanced upwards then let out a terrible screech of fear.

'The Detective Inspector!' he shouted. 'No! No! Back to the ship!'

And he took off, racing desperately for the jetty and for *Pirate Promise*, forgetting all about the fridge, the frost-house and the tingleberries.

Saracen also began running once more, but this time he was the one who was doing the chasing. They sped back past the cows, past the sandpit, still full of moaning pirates, and down to the end of the jetty. This proved tricky. They were forced to leap not only across the loose boards but over all those pirates who had been stunned at the beginning of the chase.

And what was this? *Pirate Promise* was no longer at the end of the jetty. While Grudge-Gallows was chasing Saracen, the Baconville launch had puttered past the Burnt Toast Rocks. Now it was busy towing *Pirate Promise* out into Porridge Bay. This was quite easy because the pirates hadn't bothered to drop anchor.

'Bring that ship back!' Grudge-Gallows yelled. 'Bring it back at once.'

'Come and get it!' shouted the captain of the launch.

At the sound of the captain's voice Saracen leaped back a step, carelessly landing on a loose board himself. It sprang up and struck him on the ear, but he was already so shocked and bewildered that he barely noticed. He had just heard the voice of the launch captain for the first time. He could not be mistaken. *It was the voice of the operator of the Baconville telephone exchange.*

'Grudge-Gallows, I arrest you in the name of the law!' shouted the detective inspector, Saracen's very own grandmother, flourishing her sword as the albatrosses lowered her on to the jetty.

'Keep your distance!' snarled Grudge-Gallows. He held the golden telephone high in the air. 'Or I will throw this golden telephone into the deep water at the end of the jetty. Then, even if the sharks don't swallow it, it will sink down, down, down . . . lost for ever both to you and the telephone company.'

At this very moment a phone began to ring somewhere. It wasn't the golden phone. It was Grudge-Gallows' own cell phone, slung on his belt beside his pirate cutlass.

Holding the golden phone with one hand, Grudge-Gallows pulled out the cell phone, just as a cowboy draws a six-shooter.

'Hello! Who's ringing at this vital point in my career?'

'This is the captain of the Baconville launch,' said a beautiful voice on the other end of the line. 'On behalf of the telephone company, I demand that you surrender that stolen cell phone.'

'This cell phone is mine!' shouted Grudge-Gallows. 'I am an executive pirate.' And, as he spoke, he carelessly stepped on to the last loose board on the jetty . . . a particularly wide one. It didn't spring up. Instead, it tilted slowly but surely, sliding the distracted pirate into the deep sea below.

'Through now!' cried the beautiful voice coming out of the cell phone as it flew through the air into the open hands of the detective inspector. But the gold telephone flew in the opposite direction. Glittering and gleaming, it curved out over the sea.

'My prisoner!' screamed the detective inspector as Grudge-Gallows vanished.

'My telephone!' yelled Saracen. But, just as it seemed that the gold phone was about to vanish for ever in the depths of the sea at the end of the jetty, a giant albatross (one of the few birds in the world with enough strength to carry a solid gold telephone) swooped down and swept it to safety.

'Help! Help!' Grudge-Gallows screamed, bobbing about in the deep water. 'I can't swim!'

'Now is the time to learn,' Granny shouted down to him. But Saracen did not hesitate. He dived into the deep, spun Grudge-Gallows over on to his back, seized him by his large ears and, doing a skilful frog-kick, began towing the sodden pirate towards the shore.

Chapter 22

Grudge-Gallows Begs for Mercy

Something went *putt-putt-putt* beside Saracen.
'Name and number?' murmured the voice of the captain, leaning over the side of the launch, and smiling sweetly down at Saracen.

'Can it be true? Are you the telephone operator in Baconville as well as captain of the launch?' cried Saracen, holding Grudge-Gallows by the ears and frog-kicking vigorously.

'I am,' she said. 'My grandfather taught me to operate both the telephone and the launch. I have an ocean-going mariner's certificate as well.'

'So, you didn't say you were going out to your *lunch*!' burbled Saracen, kicking hard and managing to keep Grudge-Gallows' nose above water most of the time. 'You said you were going out to your *launch*. Pretty cool! But doesn't your grandfather *ever* take a turn with the launch or the telephone?'

'Not him!' the beautiful girl replied. 'You see, until he returned he used to be a detective . . . the well-known Detective Inspector Cruddington . . .

so he found running the telephone and launch service rather boring after a few years. It drove him up the wall.'

'It was just the same with my granny,' said Saracen, amazed by the coincidence. 'She was always looking out to the distant horizon and sighing.'

'So was my grandfather,' agreed the beautiful girl. 'At last I said to him, "Off you go! *I'll* run the telephone and launch service." So he took off like a bounding lion, eager to catch a few more villains –

just like the one you're rescuing there. (I must say you look very handsome doing that rescuing!) Anyhow, I've run the telephone launch service ever since.'

'How irresponsible!' spluttered Grudge-Gallows. 'Leaving all that work to a mere slip of a girl.'

'Hey, that's amazing!' Saracen said, cunningly dunking Grudge-Gallows under the water for a second or two. There is nothing like frog-kicking your way back towards the beach while holding a pirate by the ears, and talking to a beautiful girl

who holds an ocean-going mariner's certificate, to bring out a bit of boldness in a shy man. 'You know, I think we could make an amazing team,' Saracen cried. 'You with your launch, me with my tingle-berries, and both of us with telephones. I think we were meant for each other.'

'Mercy! Mercy!' screamed Grudge-Gallows, for, like all pirates, he detested affectionate conversations. They were a form of torture to him. 'Have pity on a wilted onion in the great salad of life.'

'You know,' said the beautiful girl, ignoring the screams of a pirate in torment, 'I think you're right. You be mine and I'll be yours. How about that?'

'Terrifico!' shouted Saracen over Grudge-Gallows' cries. 'And now that I'm yours, may I ask your name?'

'Forget her name!' shouted Grudge-Gallows, bubbling and spitting. 'Just get me ashore. Oh, what utter agony! I'd rather be arrested than spend another moment in this wretched, wet, salty sea, listening to a lot of soppy dalliance.'

Neither Saracen nor the lovely girl took any notice of him.

'My name is Rosalindella,' she said, leaning tenderly over the side of the launch.

'You have the most beautiful name and the most beautiful voice in the world!' Saracen shouted, bubbling a little himself as a wave broke gently over his face. 'It's such a wonderful relief to find that you are the same person as yourself. Perhaps we could even get married some day.'

'A good idea,' said Rosalindella. 'The phone company is putting both Baconville and Breakfast Island on to direct dialling quite soon, so I could move to your island. I've always wanted to live on an island. Let's make it a date.'

'Ah! Ah! I can't stand this!' yelled Grudge-Gallows. As they reached the beach he broke free from Saracen, staggered forward a few steps and fell writhing at the feet of Saracen's granny.

'Arrest me! Arrest me!' he screamed. 'Put me in prison for twenty years. I will be a reformed man from now on. I'll concentrate on embroidery and will not hope to get time off except for good behaviour. Anything rather than listening to soppy proposals!'

The detective inspector was rather disappointed at missing a chance to use her old sword, but, since Grudge-Gallows had surrendered, she was forced to content herself with slapping handcuffs on him.

'I've brought a big fishing net to wrap around the other fourteen pirates,' said Rosalindella. 'Saracen ordered it by phone,' she added proudly.

'We'll make a detective inspector of you yet,' cried his granny clapping Saracen on the back so powerfully she almost knocked him over.

'A golden telephone is a sort of medal,' Saracen replied. 'You said I would never have any fun, or fall in love, or make a fortune. But I've done every-thing you said I would never do, and even some-thing I said I would never do, right here on the island, *and* I've caught Grudge-Gallows into the bargain. Thank you for all your good advice,

Granny, but you can save it for Detective Inspector Cruddington. I am now a crisp cucumber in the great salad of life, and I shall take my own advice from now on. I'm sticking with frost-houses, the garden and a good launch service. With these things, along with a reliable phone and the most beautiful girl in the world (who happens to have an ocean-going mariner's licence), fortune and fun will beat a way to my door, and I will open that door wide and let them in without the slightest trace of shyness. And now let's have a treat. Let's have tingleberries. There are enough for everyone, including the pirates.'

Chapter 23

Quite Another Story

On Breakfast Island beach, sitting on sand as crisp and golden as cornflakes, Saracen, Rosalindella and the detective inspector (not to mention the albatrosses and pirates) enjoyed their tingleberries. The albatrosses clacked their beaks with pleasure, and the pirates were heard to murmur to each other, 'Oh, if only my mother had fed me on tingleberries when I was an infant, I would never have embarked on a life of crime.'

'Hear that?' muttered the detective inspector, jogging Saracen with her elbow. 'Perhaps you should supply tingleberries to the Repentance Department of the Hookywalker Prison. Then Repentance would soon be more popular than the sewing class.'

'Do! Do! It would! It would!' cried Grudge-Gallows, trying to appear highly repentant. All the same, if you had happened to be looking at him as he said this, you would have seen a particularly piratical gleam in his eye as he reached greedily for his twenty-third tingleberry.

But Saracen and Rosalindella were not looking at him. They were staring out to sea. The ocean, streaked crimson and gold with the sunset, looked exactly like the juice of stewed plums. Beyond the Burnt Toast Rocks the great stewed plum of the sun itself sank slowly out of sight.

'I'm almost sorry this adventure is over,' Saracen said with a sigh.

At that exact moment, the golden telephone began to ring so loudly that everyone jumped, looking at it in alarm.

Saracen picked up the receiver. Strange noises came over the line. He distinctly heard camels coughing and the gurgle of at least one hungry vulture.

'Saracen Hobday here,' he said politely.

'This is Detective Inspector Cruddington,' groaned a weak voice. 'I'm in the middle of a sandstorm, just where the Jackrabbit Desert meets the sea, and I'm being fired at by bandits and brooded over by vultures. I desperately need help. Do you think your grandmother could rush over as soon as possible and rescue me?'

'I'm sure she'd love to,' said Saracen. 'She enjoys a good rescue. I'll pass on the message.'

'Oh, thank you, thank you!' cried Detective Inspector Cruddington.

'But while we're talking, I'd better mention that your granddaughter and I are probably going to be married when Baconville goes on to direct dialling,' Saracen went on boldly, as if he had never known what it was to be shy.

'But you are supposed to ask me for her hand in marriage,' said Detective Inspector Cruddington, sounding annoyed, though this may well have been because the bandits were still firing at him.

'A girl who has been left to run Baconville Launch Service without any help can make up her own mind,' replied Saracen rather sternly.

'Oh, all right!' muttered Detective Inspector Cruddington. 'I'll send you an engagement present. How about a cutting of a completely new plant? I found one in the desert the other day, and I think it would grow well at egg-frying temperature. I've named it the tuckertub. Expect a cutting by the vulture network . . . if I'm ever rescued, that is. So, please, please let me speak to your delightful grandmother. I am desperate.'

Granny snatched the phone from Saracen. She listened intently to Cruddington, snapped out a few comforting words, then slammed down the receiver.

'I need immediate transport beyond the albatross realm,' she cried to Grudge-Gallows and his crew. 'Help me, and we'll say no more about your trying to pirate my grandson's golden telephone.' And to Saracen she added, 'Give me a supply of tingleberries. That will ensure the crew behaves properly.'

A mere ten minutes later, the Good (or rather, the Bad) Ship, *Pirate Promise*, loaded down with enthusiastic pirates and boxes of tingleberries, set off for dangerous, desert lands. Away it sailed across Porridge Bay and past the Burnt Toast Rocks, leaving the creamy scent of tingleberries on the breeze behind it. Saracen and Rosalindella followed in the launch, waving and cheering. But as soon as *Pirate Promise* surged through the Marmalade Heads and into the open sea, the launch turned round and went back to Breakfast Island.

'You know,' Saracen said to Rosalindella, 'I might even go to Hookywalker myself. I'd like to look around the fruit and flower markets, and I might order a heater which would bring the inside of one of my glass-houses to egg-frying temperature.' There is nothing like an invasion of pirates to help a man get over his shyness.

Anyhow, those very pirates, along with Saracen's grandmother, must have reached the

Jackrabbit Desert and solved Cruddington's bandit problem in record time, because a few days later, a vulture landed at Saracen's back door with the cutting of a most amazing plant in its hooked beak. It was cactus-shaped and tasted like melted chocolate poured over raspberries, and it grew well at egg-frying temperature.

But that, of course, is another story.